ISLAND HERITAGE™
P U B L I S H I N G
A DIVISION OF THE MADDEN CORPORATION

94-411 Kō'aki Street, Waipahu, Hawai'i 96797-2806
Orders: (800) 468-2800 • Information: (808) 564-8800
Fax: (808) 564-8877
islandheritage.com

ISBN 1-59700-601-7

First Edition, Eleventh Printing - 2016

COP161101

HŌKŪ
The Stargazer

Written by Ellie Crowe & Juliet Fry • Illustrated by Kristi Petosa Sigel

Dedication:

To Sydney

-Ellie & Juliet

ISLAND HERITAGE™
PUBLISHING

Aloha! I'm Hōkū. This is my puppy, Poki, and this is my sailing canoe, the Hōkūlani—Heavenly Star.

Look! Poki found a bottle on the beach. There's a message in the bottle! It reads: PLEASE SAVE ME! I'M SHIPWRECKED ON THE FAR-AWAY NORTH ISLAND. Signed, JAKE.

Oh no! Our surfer friend, Jake, is in trouble. We have to save him!

Do you want to come on an adventure with me? Luckily, we're stargazers. The stars will guide us to the North Island. First, we have to look at the sky and find the seven stars that make up the Little Dipper. Can you help me find the brightest star in the Little Dipper's handle? There it is! It's the North Star. The North Star will be our guiding star tonight.

Now, let's wish upon a star. Star light, star bright, brightest star I see tonight, I wish I may, I wish I might, find the faraway North Island tonight. Up with the sails and we're on our way.

We're sailing through the Sea of Storms. What a wild place! The Hōkūlani is riding the waves. See the lightning flash! Listen to the thunder boom!

Poki is hiding under his blanket in our snug little cabin. The North Star is peeking through the clouds and helping us on our way. It's a sailor's special star friend. Poki has a special star friend too— he's waving his paw at Sirius, the Dog Star.

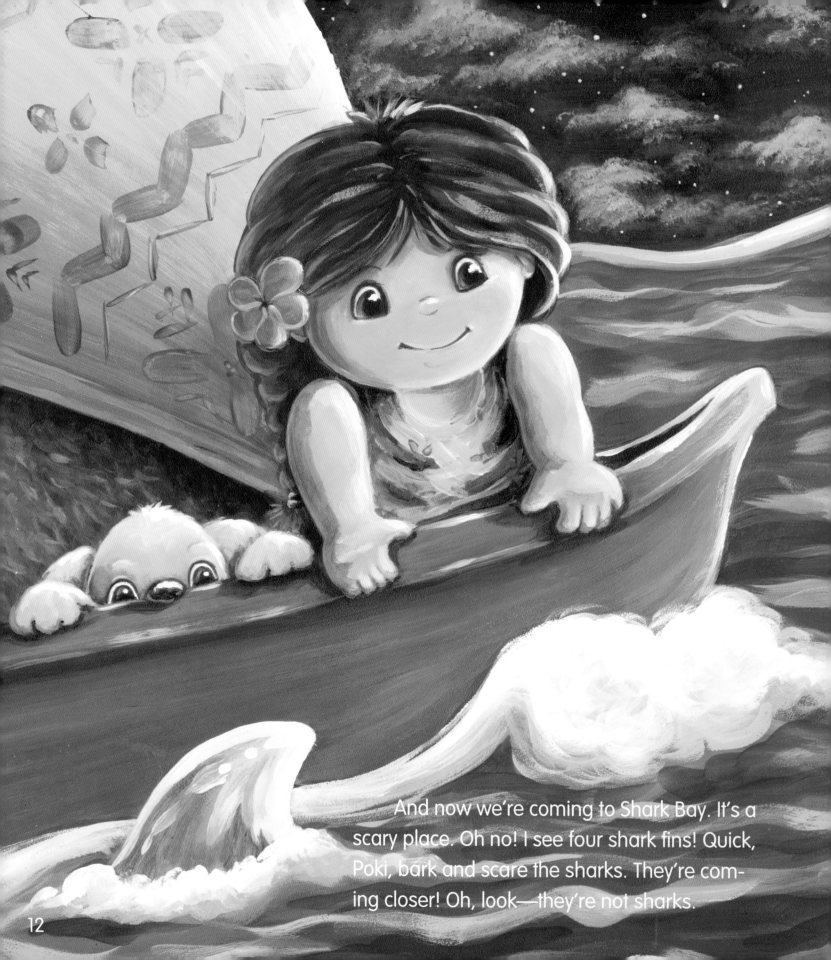

And now we're coming to Shark Bay. It's a scary place. Oh no! I see four shark fins! Quick, Poki, bark and scare the sharks. They're coming closer! Oh, look—they're not sharks.

It's Nai'a, the baby dolphin, and his friends. Hullo, Nai'a. Aloha!

13

Oooh, we're sailing past Shipwreck Sea. There are lots of sharp rocks here. And lots of wrecked ships. Long ago, Toobad the Pirate was shipwrecked on that spiky rock over there. Toobad is kind of mean. I hope he doesn't see us.

Why is Poki barking at that sailing ship? Stop barking, Poki, that's just a nice sailing ship with friendly sailors.

14

Oh no! That sailing ship has a flag with a skull and crossbones. It must be a pirate ship. It's Toobad the Pirate. If we don't sail fast, we'll soon be fish bait. Hoist the sails! Toobad is getting so close I can smell his fishy toes.

Poki, stop that growling! You're making me very nervous. Ooh, look at that humongous fin. It's Manō, the giant shark. Manō is chasing us. And Toobad is chasing us too. We have to get out of here!

Oh, good! Yes! Manō is circling
Toobad's ship. He thinks Toobad's toes smell
yummy. Toobad is sailing away as fast as he can.
Bye-bye, Toobad. Too bad about your smelly toes!

19

Away we go! We must be coming to an island. I see clouds gathering over there. And birds flying in to shore. And coconut trees. There's Jake! He's paddling out to meet us on his surfboard. He looks really happy to see us. Trim the sails. Let's surf in to meet him. Poki is a real surfer puppy!

I'm so glad we found the faraway North Island. We've been sailing all night and we're starving. Let's have a lūʻau. Can you help me spot some ripe, yellow bananas and red mangoes in the forest? Jake is climbing a coconut tree to pick a coconut. I love to drink creamy coconut milk right out of the coconut shell. Yummy! Ono!

Wasn't that a fun adventure! Thank you for helping me. Now we'll jump on the Hōkūlani and sail back home again. Away we go. And then we'll go on another adventure. Hana hou!

Sailing, sailing,
over the bounding main.
Many a stormy wind will blow
before we're home again.
Sailing, sailing,
over the waves so high.
Wherever we are, we look for a star,
we follow the stars in the sky.

The End

Author's Note:

Around a thousand years ago, Polynesians built big voyaging canoes and sailed across the vast Pacific ocean without any maps or navigational instruments. Navigators of long ago used their knowledge of the paths of stars rising or setting to find their way. They were guided also by other direction indicators such as dominant ocean swells. The presence of islands could be detected by the sight of drifting flotsam, the flight paths of sea birds, and gathered cloud masses, sometimes reflecting bright lagoons. The amazing navigators of long ago were called star gazers and way finders. In 1976, a brave group of sailors from Hawai'i built a voyaging canoe, Hōkūle'a (Star of Gladness), and sailed it more than 2,500 miles from Hawai'i to Tahiti guided by the stars and ocean signs just like the Polynesians of long ago.